Life Under the Sea

Sea Horses

by Cari Meister

Bullfrog Books

Ideas for Parents and Teachers

Bullfrog Books let children practice reading informational text at the earliest reading levels. Repetition, familiar words, and photo labels support early readers.

Before Reading

- Ask the child to think about sea horses. Ask: What do you know about sea horses?
- Look at the picture glossary together. Read and discuss the words.

Read the Book

- Read the book to the child, or have him or her read independently.
- Point out the photo labels to reinforce new vocabulary as you read.

After Reading

- Prompt the child to think more. Ask: How does being able to change color help a sea horse? What would it be like to live under water?

Bullfrog Books are published by Jump!
5357 Penn Avenue South
Minneapolis, MN 55419
www.jumplibrary.com

Library of Congress Cataloging-in-Publication Data
Meister, Cari.
Sea horses / by Cari Meister.
p. cm. -- (Bullfrog books. Life under the sea)
Summary: "This photo-illustrated book for early readers tells the story of sea horses finding a mate and having babies"-- Provided by publisher.
Audience: 005.
Audience: K to grade 3.
Includes bibliographical references and index.
ISBN 978-1-62031-033-5 (hardcover : alk. paper) --
ISBN 978-1-62496-051-2 (ebook)
1. Sea horses--Juvenile literature. 2. Sea horses--Behavior--Juvenile literature. I. Title.
QL638.S9M44 2014
597'.6798--dc23 2013001959

Series Editor Rebecca Glaser
Book Designer Ellen Huber
Photo Researcher Heather Dreisbach

Photo Credits: Alamy, 4, 14; Corbis, 6, 16–17, 19, 23bl; Dreamstime, 8–9, 15, 18, 24; Getty, 7; iStockPhoto, 10–11; National Geographic, 20, 21, 23tr, Shutterstock, cover, 1, 3l, 3r, 12–13, 22, 23tl, 23br; SuperStock, 5

Printed in the United States of America at Corporate Graphics, North Mankato, Minnesota.
5-2013 / PO 1003

10 9 8 7 6 5 4 3 2 1

Table of Contents

Looking for a Mate

In the warm ocean, a sea horse looks for his mate.

He looks like a horse.
But he is a fish.

He has gills.

They help
him breathe.

Wait! There is danger.

A crab!

The seahorse grabs sea grass with his tail.

He turns the color of grass.

Now he blends in.

He is safe.

Here comes his mate! Do you see her dorsal fin?

It helps her swim.

Do you see her pectoral fin?

It helps her turn.

Sea horses swim in pairs.

They hook their tails.

Time to dance!

Sea horses have a long mating dance.

Then, the female drops eggs into the male's brood pouch.

He grows the eggs.

Soon, babies are born.

Parts of a Sea Horse

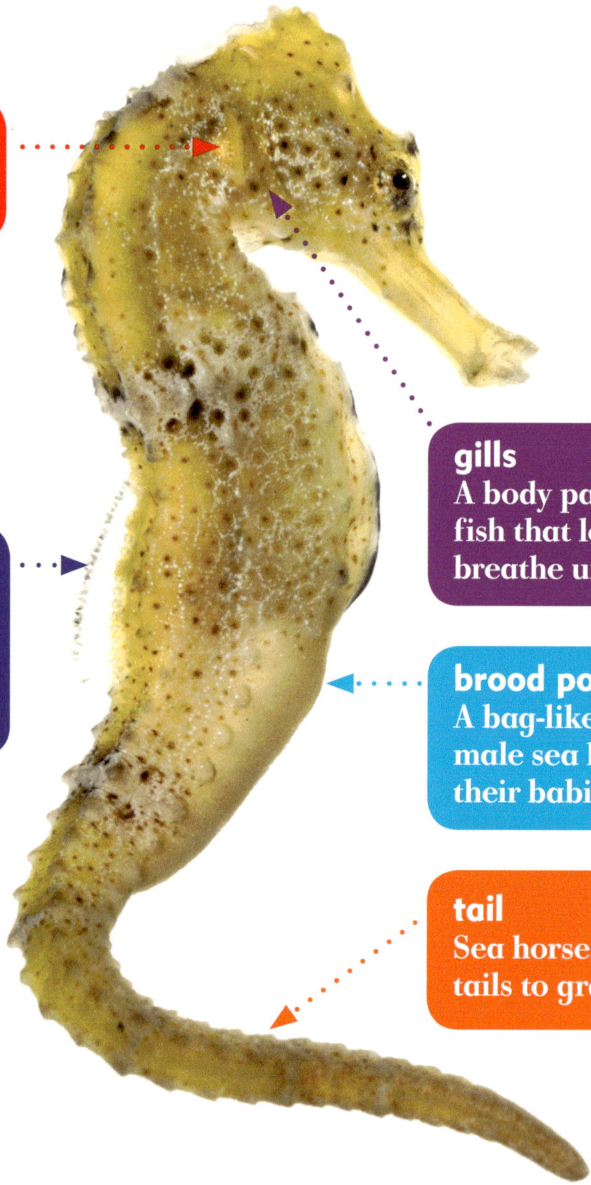

pectoral fin
A fin that helps with steering.

dorsal fin
A fin on the back of a fish that helps it balance and swim.

gills
A body part in a fish that lets it breathe under water.

brood pouch
A bag-like pocket in male sea horses where their babies grow.

tail
Sea horses use their tails to grab things.

Picture Glossary

crab
A type of ocean animal with a hard shell, eight legs, and two claws.

mating dance
When a male and female sea horse swim around together and get ready to lay eggs.

mate
A fish's partner; a sea horse needs a mate to make babies.

sea grass
A type of grass that grows in salt water.

Index

To Learn More

Learning more is as easy as 1, 2, 3.

1) Go to www.factsurfer.com

2) Enter "sea horse" into the search box.

3) Click the "Surf" button to see a list of websites.

With factsurfer.com, finding more information is just a click away.